SHARDS OF STRENGTH

ADDICTION

POONAM PACHOURI

Copyright © Poonam Pachouri
All Rights Reserved.

This book has been self-published with all reasonable efforts taken to make the material error-free by the author. No part of this book shall be used, reproduced in any manner whatsoever without written permission from the author, except in the case of brief quotations embodied in critical articles and reviews.

The Author of this book is solely responsible and liable for its content including but not limited to the views, representations, descriptions, statements, information, opinions and references ["Content"]. The Content of this book shall not constitute or be construed or deemed to reflect the opinion or expression of the Publisher or Editor. Neither the Publisher nor Editor endorse or approve the Content of this book or guarantee the reliability, accuracy or completeness of the Content published herein and do not make any representations or warranties of any kind, express or implied, including but not limited to the implied warranties of merchantability, fitness for a particular purpose. The Publisher and Editor shall not be liable whatsoever for any errors, omissions, whether such errors or omissions result from negligence, accident, or any other cause or claims for loss or damages of any kind, including without limitation, indirect or consequential loss or damage arising out of use, inability to use, or about the reliability, accuracy or sufficiency of the information contained in this book.

Made with ♥ on the Notion Press Platform
www.notionpress.com

Introduction

In the shadows of a broken home, where silence often speaks louder than words, lies a story of survival, resilience, and the unyielding strength of the human spirit. *Shards of Strength* is a deeply personal tale that delves into the turbulent life of Anand Patel, a young boy navigating the emotional wreckage of his father's alcohol abuse.

Set against the backdrop of a modest Indian city, this novel explores the harrowing reality of domestic violence and its profound impact on a family. It is a story not just about the pain and fear inflicted by an abusive household, but about the quiet acts of courage that can lead to liberation and healing.

At the heart of this narrative is the bond between Anand and his mother, Priya, who together shoulder the weight of survival while protecting Meera, Anand's younger sister, from the harshest edges of their reality. As Anand pours his emotions into poetry and Priya dreams of rebuilding her life through a small food stall, the Patel family begins to rediscover hope amidst despair.

But the road to freedom is never easy. *Shards of Strength* examines the societal stigma, economic challenges, and emotional scars that linger long after the physical chains are broken. It is a story that captures the complexity of healing and the power of family to reclaim their lives, even in the face of overwhelming odds.

For anyone who has ever felt trapped by circumstances beyond their control, for those who have fought to find light in the darkest corners, this novel is a testament to resilience. Anand's journey reminds us that even when the world feels broken, there is always a way forward—a way to gather the shards of our past and build something beautiful.

Let this story inspire you, challenge you, and remind you of the unbreakable strength within us all

• iv •

CHAPTER ONE

Shattered Silence

The clock on the wall ticked loudly, the only sound in the dim, suffocating silence of the Patel family's apartment. It was almost midnight, and Anand Patel lay wide awake on his bed, staring at the ceiling, waiting for the storm he knew was coming. He didn't know why he still felt the need to brace himself—he'd seen the same storm play out countless times before. His father, Rajesh, would stumble through the door, drunk and volatile, his anger ignited by nothing more than the slightest imagined provocation.

Anand turned his head toward the door, hearing the unmistakable shuffle of unsteady feet on the stairs outside. The building's flimsy walls did nothing to mask the sound of Rajesh muttering to himself, a mix of curses and incoherent grievances. Anand's chest tightened as the key rattled in the lock.

The door swung open, and there he was. Rajesh stood in the doorway, his hair disheveled, his shirt untucked, and his eyes bloodshot. The strong smell of alcohol hit Anand even before his father spoke. "Priya!" Rajesh bellowed, slamming the door shut behind him.

Anand froze, listening to his mother's hurried footsteps as she emerged from the kitchen. She tried to greet Rajesh calmly, her voice low and soothing. "You're home late. Let me get you some water."

But Rajesh wasn't looking for water—or peace. "Don't pretend to care, Priya," he sneered, his voice slurred. "You don't do anything for this family. Just sit around all day waiting for me to fix everything."

"That's not true," Priya said softly, her tone pleading. "I'm trying—"

"Trying?" Rajesh interrupted, his voice rising. "Trying to what? Make me look like a fool? You think you're better than me?"

From his room, Anand clenched his fists, his body tense. He wanted to intervene, to protect his mother, but he knew it would only make things worse. The last time he'd tried, Rajesh had turned his rage on him, and Anand still remembered the sting of his father's slap.

Beside him, Meera stirred in her sleep. She was only eight, far too young to understand the complexity of what was happening, but old enough to sense the danger. She rolled over, her face scrunching in discomfort, and Anand instinctively placed a hand on her shoulder to calm her.

"It's okay," he whispered, though he didn't believe his own words.

The shouting in the living room grew louder. Anand could hear Rajesh pacing, the sound of his shoes scuffing against the floor. Then came the crash—something fragile, a glass or plate, smashing against the wall. Meera woke with a start, her eyes wide with fear.

"Is he mad again?" she asked, her voice trembling.

Anand nodded, his jaw tight. "Just stay here. Don't move."

In the living room, Priya tried to clean up the broken glass, her hands trembling. "You don't need to do this," she said softly, her voice almost breaking.

Rajesh sneered. "Don't tell me what I need to do. You think you're in charge? You can't even handle your own kids!"

Anand felt his heart hammering in his chest. He couldn't take it anymore. He got up from the bed, but before he could leave the room, Meera grabbed his arm. "Don't go, bhaiya," she begged, tears streaming down her face. "Please don't go."

He hesitated, torn between his protective instincts and the fear of escalating the situation. Rajesh's voice echoed in his ears, growing angrier by the second. Anand knew he couldn't change anything—not tonight.

Instead, he sat back down beside Meera, pulling her into a hug. "It's okay," he whispered again, stroking her hair as she sobbed quietly. "I'm here. I won't let anything happen to you."

As the shouting continued, Anand's mind raced. He thought about the glass on the floor, the tears in his mother's eyes, the fear etched into Meera's face. He thought about the promises Rajesh used to make—the father who once lifted him onto his shoulders, telling him he'd be a great man someday. That man was gone, replaced by the broken shell who now terrorized their home.

Anand clenched his fists tighter, his nails digging into his palms. He couldn't let this continue. He didn't know how, but he had to find a way to protect his mother and sister. He had to find a way to escape.

The clock struck midnight, the ticking growing louder in the silence that followed Rajesh's final outburst. The apartment was still again, save for the sound of Meera's soft breathing as she drifted back to sleep in Anand's arms. He lay awake, staring at the ceiling, his resolve hardening like steel.

Tomorrow, he thought. Tomorrow, I'll figure something out.

CHAPTER TWO

The Mask at School

The morning sunlight filtered through the thin curtains of Anand's room, but it felt more oppressive than uplifting. He hadn't slept much, his mind still replaying the events of the previous night. Meera stirred beside him, her small body curled against his as if seeking protection from nightmares. Anand stroked her hair softly, waiting until she woke.

When she finally opened her eyes, her face brightened momentarily, forgetting the turmoil of the night before. "Do I have to go to school today?" she asked, her voice still groggy.

"Yes, Meera," Anand said gently, helping her sit up. "We have to keep going, no matter what." He didn't add that school was her only refuge from the storm of their home life.

By the time they reached their school, the hum of students' chatter surrounded them. Anand walked Meera to her class, crouching to fix her loose shoelace. "You're safe here," he whispered, smiling at her. She nodded, though her grip on his hand lingered for a moment before she disappeared into her classroom.

Anand trudged toward his own building, the weight of the world pressing on his shoulders. The sound of laughter and lockers slamming felt distant, like a world he didn't belong to.

His classmates didn't know about his bruises, both physical and emotional, and he preferred it that way.

In English class, Ms. Thomas began discussing a poem about resilience. Anand stared at his notebook, not listening. His mind drifted back to the glass shattering against the wall the night before. His father's slurred voice echoed in his head: "You think you're better than me? You're nothing."

"Anand?" Ms. Thomas's voice broke through his thoughts.

He looked up, startled.

"Can you explain what the poet means by finding strength in silence?" she asked, her tone soft but insistent.

Anand froze. His classmates turned to look at him, and he felt their curiosity piercing him like needles. He opened his mouth to speak but couldn't find the words. His silence stretched uncomfortably long.

"That's okay," Ms. Thomas said, moving on to another student. But her eyes lingered on him for a moment, filled with something he couldn't quite place—concern, perhaps.

After class, Ms. Thomas called him to her desk. Anand hesitated, unsure whether to stay or flee. Finally, he approached her, his hands shoved into his pockets.

"You've been quiet lately," she said. "Is everything okay at home?"

Her words hit him like a punch to the gut. For a moment, he wanted to tell her everything—the shouting, the fear, the bruises his mother tried to hide. But he couldn't. He shook his head.

"Everything's fine," he said, his voice barely above a whisper.

Ms. Thomas studied him, her eyes gentle but probing. "If you ever need to talk, Anand, I'm here."

He nodded quickly and walked away, her words bouncing around in his mind. For the rest of the day, he buried himself in silence, his mask firmly in place.

CHAPTER THREE

Shadows at Home

When Anand and Meera returned home that afternoon, the apartment felt eerily still. Rajesh was gone, probably out drinking again. Priya sat at the kitchen table, staring blankly at a cup of tea that had long since gone cold.

"Hi, Ma," Anand said softly, placing his school bag on the floor. Priya glanced up at him, her face pale and drawn.

"How was school?" she asked, her voice hollow.

"It was fine," he lied. He moved closer to her, noticing the dark circles under her eyes and the faint bruise on her wrist. His stomach twisted.

"Did… did he hurt you again?" Anand asked, his voice trembling.

Priya flinched slightly, then shook her head. "No. It's fine, Anand. He just had too much to drink."

Her words made Anand's blood boil. "Too much to drink? Ma, he threw a glass at you! How can you just brush that off?"

Priya looked down, her fingers gripping the edge of the table. "What choice do I have?" she whispered. "He's your father, Anand. We can't just leave him."

"Yes, we can!" Anand said, his voice rising. "We can't keep living like this. It's killing you, Ma. It's killing all of us."

Priya shook her head, tears welling in her eyes. "Where would we go? We have no money, no family to take us in. At least here we have a roof over our heads."

Anand opened his mouth to argue but stopped. Deep down, he knew she was right. They had nothing—no savings, no relatives who would help them. The system was built against people like them.

Meera walked into the room, holding a piece of paper. "Look what I drew!" she said, her voice bright and hopeful.

Anand took the drawing and smiled faintly. It was a picture of their family, but instead of their cramped apartment, they were standing in a bright, sunny park. Everyone was smiling, even Rajesh.

"It's beautiful, Meera," Anand said, ruffling her hair.

Priya glanced at the drawing, her tears spilling over. "It's nice, sweetheart," she said softly, her voice breaking.

That night, after putting Meera to bed, Anand sat in his room, staring at his notebook. He picked up his pen and began to write:

"The walls are thin, but the silence is thinner.
Bruises fade, but the scars remain.
We smile for a future that feels like a dream,
But dreams don't come true in houses of shadows."

He closed the notebook, his chest heavy with frustration. He wanted to protect his mother and sister, but he didn't know how. The world felt stacked against them, a maze with no escape. But one thought burned brightly in his mind: he had to find a way out—no matter what it took.

CHAPTER FOUR

Verses in the Dark

Late at night, Anand sat on his bed, the dim glow of a single bulb illuminating his small room. Outside, the city had fallen quiet, but the stillness in their apartment was heavy. Meera was asleep beside him, her small figure curled under a worn blanket. Across the hall, Priya's muffled cries broke through the fragile silence. She was alone in the kitchen, no doubt reliving the night's argument, the fear, and the bruises she hid so well.

Anand clenched his fists, anger bubbling inside him. He couldn't stand feeling helpless, unable to protect the two people he loved most. He opened his notebook, the only place he could pour out the storm inside him. The first lines came slowly, tentative, but soon the words began to flow:

"In the shadows of a house that isn't home,
We wear silence like armor,
But the noise inside never sleeps.
A mother's tears, a sister's innocence,
A boy's dreams turned to dust."

He paused, staring at the page. The words felt too raw, too real, but he couldn't stop. Writing was the only thing that made him feel in control, the only way to process the chaos of his world. He thought about his father's words—angry, cutting, accusing. The memories stung, but they also fueled his resolve.

"I am more than the echoes of his rage.
I am more than his failure."

The thought made him pause. Was he really more than this life? Could he ever escape the cycle of fear and anger that surrounded him? He didn't know. But he wanted to believe it was possible—for his mother's sake, for Meera's.

The clock ticked past midnight as he finished the poem. He closed the notebook and leaned back against the wall, staring at the ceiling. In the quiet, he could hear Meera's soft breathing and the faint hum of the refrigerator in the kitchen. He wished he could bottle this rare moment of peace and make it last forever.

But he knew better. Morning would come, and with it, Rajesh would return, bringing his anger and the stench of alcohol. The storm was always waiting, just beyond the horizon.

Before turning off the light, Anand whispered to himself, "One day, we'll get out of here. One day, I'll make things better."

CHAPTER FIVE

The Breaking Point

It was a Saturday evening when the storm finally broke. Rajesh had been drinking since the afternoon, his mood swinging from sullen to volatile. Priya tried to keep Meera busy in the living room, hoping to shield her from his rage, but the tension in the air was palpable. Anand sat at the table, pretending to do homework, but his eyes were on Rajesh.

"You think you're so clever, don't you?" Rajesh sneered, his bloodshot eyes fixed on Anand. "Sitting there with your books, acting like you're better than me."

Anand gritted his teeth, refusing to respond. He'd learned long ago that answering only made things worse.

"Answer me!" Rajesh bellowed, slamming his fist on the table.

"Rajesh, stop," Priya said softly, stepping between them.

Her intervention only fueled his anger. "Don't tell me what to do!" he shouted, shoving her aside. Priya stumbled but caught herself, her face pale with fear.

Something inside Anand snapped. He stood up, his heart pounding. "Leave her alone!" he shouted, his voice shaking but defiant.

Rajesh turned to him, his expression darkening. "You think you're a man now?" he snarled. Before Anand could move, Rajesh slapped him hard across the face. The impact sent him reeling, his cheek stinging with pain.

Meera screamed, running to Priya, who pulled her close. Rajesh stepped back, his chest heaving, as if even he was surprised by what he'd done. Anand straightened slowly, his fists clenched, his eyes burning with anger.

"Don't touch her again," he said through gritted teeth.

For a moment, the room was silent. Then Rajesh sneered. "You're just a boy," he said, his voice dripping with contempt. "You don't know anything about what it means to be a man."

Anand didn't respond. He turned and walked toward his room, his jaw tight. He could hear Priya trying to calm Rajesh, her voice trembling. The sound made him feel sick.

That night, Anand sat in his room, the left side of his face throbbing. Meera was asleep on his bed, her tear-streaked face buried in the pillow. Anand stared at the notebook on his desk, but for once, the words wouldn't come.

The anger and helplessness churned inside him like a storm. He thought about the way Rajesh had looked at Priya, the way he'd spoken to her, and the way she'd tried so hard to protect Meera. How much longer could she endure this? How much longer could any of them?

Anand knew he couldn't stay silent anymore. Something had to change. He didn't know how to fix everything, but he had to try.

The first step came to him like a whisper in the back of his mind: **write it down. Share the truth. Make the world see what's happening.**

The thought scared him, but it also gave him a strange sense of purpose. For the first time in a long time, Anand felt like he had a plan.

As he leaned back against the wall, his face still stinging, he whispered to himself, "This ends here."

CHAPTER SIX

A Ray of Light

Anand sat at his desk in the back of the English classroom, trying to focus on the lesson. Ms. Thomas was introducing a new writing assignment about resilience, and her voice carried an energy that usually drew the class in. But Anand wasn't listening. His mind was still back at home, replaying the slap, the shouting, and his mother's quiet tears.

"Anand?" Ms. Thomas's voice broke through his thoughts. He looked up, startled.

"Sorry," he mumbled.

Ms. Thomas frowned but moved on, her gaze lingering on him for a moment. At the end of class, she approached his desk. "Stay after for a moment, Anand," she said softly.

He hesitated but nodded, waiting until the other students had filed out. Ms. Thomas sat on the edge of her desk, folding her arms. "You've been distracted lately," she said. "Your grades are slipping, and you seem… somewhere else. What's going on?"

Anand's chest tightened. He wanted to tell her, to let the truth spill out, but fear held him back. What if she didn't believe him? What if it only made things worse at home?

"I'm fine," he said quickly, avoiding her gaze.

Ms. Thomas studied him for a moment, then picked up a notebook from her desk. "You left this behind last week," she said, handing it to him. Anand froze. It was his notebook—the one where he wrote everything he couldn't say aloud.

"I read some of it," Ms. Thomas admitted, her voice gentle. "Your words are powerful, Anand. They're raw and honest, and I can tell they come from a place of pain."

Anand felt exposed, like a spotlight was shining on him. He wanted to snatch the notebook and run, but Ms. Thomas's next words stopped him.

"I grew up in a home like yours," she said quietly. "My father drank. He hurt my mom, and sometimes he hurt me too. Writing was how I survived it."

Anand stared at her, stunned. He'd never heard a teacher talk so openly, so vulnerably. "What happened?" he asked before he could stop himself.

Ms. Thomas smiled faintly. "We got out. It wasn't easy, but we found a way. And now, I try to help others do the same." She leaned forward. "You're stronger than you think, Anand. And your words—your voice—can make a difference."

She handed him a flyer. "There's a local writing competition coming up. The theme is survival. I think you should enter."

Anand looked at the flyer, his heart pounding. The idea terrified him, but a small spark of hope flickered inside him. Maybe his words could be more than an escape. Maybe they could be a weapon—a way to fight back.

CHAPTER SEVEN

Decisions and Doubts

That evening, Anand sat at his desk, the flyer from Ms. Thomas in one hand and his notebook in the other. The contest seemed like a lifeline, but doubt gnawed at him. What if he wasn't good enough? What if his father found out?

He opened his notebook, flipping through pages filled with raw emotions and fragmented dreams. His words felt too personal, too vulnerable to share with anyone else. But then he thought about his mother and Meera, about the nights filled with shouting and fear. They deserved better.

"Anand?" Priya's voice pulled him from his thoughts. She stood in the doorway, her face lined with exhaustion. "What are you working on?"

He hesitated, then held up the flyer. "There's a writing competition," he said. "The prize is money. I thought… maybe I could try."

Priya stepped closer, her eyes scanning the flyer. For a moment, her face softened, and she smiled. "You've always been good with words," she said. "You should do it."

Anand frowned. "What if I don't win? What if—"

Priya placed a hand on his shoulder. "It's not about winning," she said. "It's about trying. Showing the world what you're capable of. I'm proud of you, Anand."

Her words settled something inside him, a quiet reassurance that gave him the courage to open his notebook. He flipped to a blank page and began to write.

"In the echoes of a father's rage,
We found strength in each other.
In the silence of a mother's tears,
We learned to endure.
This is not the end of us."

The lines flowed easily, each one pulling him deeper into his emotions. He wrote about Meera's quiet resilience, Priya's unwavering strength, and his own determination to break free.

But as the days passed, doubt crept back in. Rajesh was unpredictable, his moods swinging wildly depending on how much he'd had to drink. Anand worried that entering the competition might anger him, might bring more chaos into their fragile lives.

One night, as Anand sat at his desk, Meera climbed onto his lap. "What are you writing?" she asked, her eyes wide with curiosity.

Anand smiled faintly. "It's a poem. For a contest."

"Will you win?" she asked.

"I don't know," he admitted.

Meera tilted her head, studying him. "You always write nice things," she said. "I think you'll win."

Her innocent faith in him made his chest ache. "Thanks, Meera," he said softly, hugging her close.

As she climbed back into bed, Anand stared at his notebook. The doubts were still there, but so was the spark of hope. He picked up his pen and wrote another line:

"We are not broken.
We are more than what tries to destroy us."

For the first time in weeks, he felt a small sense of purpose. He would finish the poem, no matter what.

CHAPTER EIGHT

The Contest Submission

The night before the competition deadline, Anand sat at his desk, his notebook open to the final draft of his poem. The words on the page felt raw and powerful, a mirror of everything he'd carried for so long. Priya had read it earlier and smiled, her eyes welling with tears. "You've captured everything," she'd said. "I'm so proud of you."

Anand felt a rare flicker of hope as he copied the poem onto the official entry form. He imagined the possibility of winning—not just the prize money, but the validation that his voice mattered. That his family's story mattered.

But just as he finished, the front door slammed open. Anand froze. Rajesh stumbled into the apartment, his eyes bloodshot and his movements erratic. The familiar stench of alcohol filled the air.

"What's this?" Rajesh slurred, snatching the entry form off the desk. Anand jumped to his feet, panic rising.

"It's nothing!" he said quickly, trying to grab it back, but Rajesh held it out of reach, squinting at the words.

"'In the echoes of rage…' What is this garbage?" Rajesh sneered, his voice rising. "You think you're some kind of writer? This won't put food on the table!"

"Please, just give it back," Anand said, his voice trembling.

Rajesh's expression twisted into anger. "You waste your time on this instead of helping your mother. You're useless, just like her!" With a sudden burst of rage, he tore the paper in half, letting the pieces fall to the floor.

"NO!" Anand shouted, lunging forward, but it was too late. The words he'd poured his heart into lay scattered in tatters.

Priya rushed into the room, her face pale. "Rajesh, stop this!" she pleaded, stepping between him and Anand.

Rajesh turned on her, his voice venomous. "You defend this? You've let him turn into a lazy dreamer!"

"Get out of here!" Priya shouted, her voice trembling with both fear and anger. For the first time, she pushed back, forcing Rajesh to stumble away from the desk.

Rajesh glared at them both before staggering into his bedroom, slamming the door behind him. The apartment fell silent, except for the sound of Priya's shallow breaths.

Anand sank to the floor, gathering the torn pieces of his poem. His hands shook as he tried to fit them back together, but the jagged edges refused to align. Priya knelt beside him, her eyes brimming with tears.

"You can rewrite it," she said softly, touching his shoulder. "You've done it once. You can do it again."

Anand stared at her, his chest heavy. "What's the point? He's right. It won't change anything."

Priya cupped his face, forcing him to look at her. "It will change something, Anand. It will remind you who you are. And that's everything."

Her words lit a small spark inside him. He nodded slowly, pulling himself together. As Priya helped him clear the desk, Anand opened his notebook and began to write again.

The clock ticked past midnight as he worked, recreating the poem from memory. Each word felt like a rebellion, a refusal to let his father's anger define him. By the time dawn broke, the poem was finished.

Priya smiled as Anand handed her the final draft. "Go submit it," she said. "And don't look back."

CHAPTER NINE

Unbroken Words

The school auditorium buzzed with chatter as students and teachers gathered for the announcement of the writing competition winner. Anand sat near the back, his hands clenched tightly in his lap. He felt exposed, as though every pair of eyes in the room could see straight into his soul.

Ms. Thomas found him before the event began, placing a reassuring hand on his shoulder. "No matter what happens, you've already won," she said. "Sharing your truth takes more courage than anything else."

Anand nodded, though his stomach churned with nerves. He glanced at Priya and Meera, who sat in the audience. Meera waved enthusiastically, her smile lighting up the room. Priya gave him a small nod, her pride evident in her tear-filled eyes.

Finally, the principal took the stage, holding an envelope in his hands. "The winner of this year's writing competition is… Anand Patel."

Anand froze as the room erupted into applause. His heart pounded as Ms. Thomas nudged him forward. Slowly, he made his way to the stage, each step feeling heavier than the last.

When he reached the podium, the principal handed him the microphone. "Anand's poem is a powerful story of resilience and hope," he said. "We're honored to hear it today."

Anand unfolded the paper in his hands, his palms damp with sweat. He took a deep breath and began to read:

"In the echoes of a father's rage,
We found strength in silence.
In the tears of a mother's fight,
We built a bridge to hope.

"Through shadows and storms,
We carry the light of tomorrow.
We are not broken.
We are unbroken."

As his voice filled the room, Anand felt the weight of his words lifting from his shoulders. The silence in the auditorium was profound, the audience hanging on every line. When he finished, the applause was deafening.

Anand stepped back from the podium, his chest heaving. He glanced at Priya and Meera, who were on their feet, clapping with unrestrained joy. For the first time, Anand felt like his words had power—not just to heal himself, but to inspire others.

After the event, students and teachers approached him, sharing their own stories of struggle. One girl, her voice trembling, said, "Your poem… it's my life, too."

Anand realized then that he wasn't alone. His pain, his truth, had connected him to something larger—a community of people fighting their own battles.

That night, as he sat at his desk, Anand opened his notebook to a fresh page. For the first time in years, the future felt less like a burden and more like a promise.

CHAPTER TEN

Freedom at Last

The apartment was quiet. Too quiet. The kind of silence that felt heavy, like it had something to say but couldn't find the words. Priya sat at the kitchen table, staring at her empty hands as if they could somehow hold the answers. The weight of years spent managing Rajesh's anger, his broken promises, and his spiraling addiction seemed to catch up with her all at once.

Across the room, Anand stood by the window, his shoulders stiff, his hands gripping the windowsill. He'd won the writing competition, poured his heart out on that stage, and yet, the triumph felt hollow. It didn't change the reality waiting for them here—the reality of a home ruled by fear.

Priya finally broke the silence. "He won't stop, Anand," she said, her voice barely audible.

Anand turned to face her, his jaw tight. "I know."

Her hands trembled as she pushed back her chair and stood, pacing the small kitchen. "I thought… maybe he'd see what he was doing to us. Maybe he'd stop. But he doesn't care. He doesn't care about us." Her voice cracked, and she pressed a hand to her mouth, trying to stifle a sob.

Anand crossed the room, placing a hand on her shoulder. "Ma, it's not your fault."

She shook her head, tears spilling down her cheeks. "I stayed too long. I let him hurt you. Hurt Meera. I thought… I thought I could fix him, but I couldn't."

"You stayed because you thought it was best for us," Anand said, his voice steady but his own emotions threatening to break through. "You didn't do this, Ma. He did."

Before Priya could respond, the front door slammed open, and Rajesh stumbled inside. The smell of alcohol hit them first, followed by his slurred voice. "What's this, huh? A little family meeting without me?"

Anand moved in front of Priya instinctively, his body tense. "Leave us alone, Dad," he said, his voice firm but trembling with anger.

Rajesh sneered. "Leave? This is my house. My family. You don't get to tell me what to do." He staggered toward them, his hands clenched into fists.

Priya stepped forward, her voice trembling but resolute. "We're leaving, Rajesh. The kids and I—we're done."

Her words stopped him in his tracks. For a moment, his face softened, and he looked almost like the man he used to be—the man who had once laughed with her, held her hand, and promised to build a life together. But the moment passed as quickly as it came, replaced by anger.

"You can't leave," he spat. "You need me. You'd be nothing without me."

Priya flinched, but Anand stood his ground. "We don't need you," he said, his voice shaking but determined. "We never did."

Rajesh lunged toward them, but before he could get close, the sound of sirens filled the air. Priya had called the police earlier, her trembling hands dialing the number when Rajesh was still out. The officers burst through the door moments later, their presence filling the small apartment.

Rajesh turned to face them, his anger flaring. "This is my house!" he shouted. "They're my family!"

One of the officers stepped forward calmly. "Sir, you need to come with us."

Rajesh resisted, shouting incoherently, but the officers subdued him quickly. As they led him out the door, he turned back to Priya, his expression a mix of rage and desperation. "You'll regret this," he spat. "You'll come crawling back."

The door closed behind him, leaving the apartment in an almost deafening silence. Priya sank to the floor, her hands covering her face as sobs wracked her body.

Anand knelt beside her, wrapping his arms around her tightly. "It's over, Ma," he whispered, his own voice breaking. "He's gone."

For a long time, they stayed like that, the weight of years of fear and pain pouring out in tears. Meera peeked out from her bedroom, her small voice breaking the quiet. "Is Daddy gone?"

Priya wiped her tears and nodded, her voice trembling but steady. "Yes, sweetheart. He's gone."

Meera ran to her, burying her face in Priya's lap. They held each other, the three of them, their broken pieces fitting together like a puzzle.

Here's the continuation of Anand's journey with **Epilogue: Rebuilding and Resilience**, focusing on the family's efforts to heal emotionally, rebuild economically, and rediscover hope.

CHAPTER ELEVEN

Epilogue: Rebuilding and Resilience

A Family's First Steps

The days that followed were filled with small but meaningful changes. Priya began attending counseling sessions at the shelter, her initial hesitance melting as she opened up about years of fear and pain. She spoke quietly but honestly about the toll Rajesh's addiction had taken on her—how she had learned to shrink herself to avoid his wrath, how she had convinced herself that staying was safer than leaving.

Each session seemed to lighten her burden just a little. She started smiling more, even laughing occasionally. Anand noticed the difference and felt a quiet sense of pride. His mother, who had endured so much, was finding her strength again.

Meera, too, began to blossom. At school, she joined an art club, where she created bright, colorful drawings that reflected the dreams she was beginning to believe in. One evening, she proudly showed Anand a picture she had drawn of their family standing in front of a sunny house surrounded by flowers.

"Do you think we'll ever have a house like this?" she asked, her eyes hopeful.

Anand knelt beside her, studying the picture. "I think we will," he said. "We just have to keep working toward it."

Anand's Path to Purpose

For Anand, writing became more than just an escape—it became his purpose. Ms. Thomas encouraged him to submit more of his work to local competitions and publications. One day, he received an email from a community magazine accepting one of his poems for publication. The accompanying note read: "Your words carry so much power. Keep writing. The world needs your voice."

Anand shared the news with Priya and Meera over dinner that night. Meera clapped her hands, her excitement contagious. Priya reached across the table, her eyes shining with pride. "You're making a difference, Anand," she said. "You're showing people that they're not alone."

The recognition gave Anand the courage to take his writing a step further. He began speaking at local community events, sharing his poems and his family's story. At first, he was nervous, his voice shaky as he stood before a room full of strangers. But as he spoke, he saw nods of understanding, tears of empathy, and smiles of encouragement. Each event felt like a small victory—not just for him, but for his mother and sister, too.

Priya's New Dream

As Anand pursued his writing, Priya found a new sense of purpose, too. She had always loved cooking—an art she had perfected even with limited resources. One evening, as they sat together at the table, Priya hesitated before speaking. "I've been thinking," she began. "What if I opened a food stall? Something small—chai, pakoras, maybe samosas. It's a risk, but I think I can make it work."

Anand's face lit up. "That's a great idea, Ma," he said. "You're an amazing cook. People will love it."

Over the next few weeks, the family worked together to make Priya's dream a reality. Anand helped design signs for the stall, while Meera added her artistic touch with bright, cheerful colors. On the day of the stall's grand opening, Priya stood behind the counter, her hands steady as she served her first customers. By the end of the day, she had sold out of everything.

"It's a start," she said that evening, her smile wider than it had been in years.

The Weight of Freedom

One night, as they sat on the small balcony of their apartment, Priya turned to Anand. "Do you think about him?" she asked quietly.

Anand knew who she meant. He leaned back in his chair, staring at the stars. "Sometimes," he admitted. "But not the man he became. I think about the father he was before…" His voice trailed off, and he shook his head. "But it doesn't matter. He's not part of our lives anymore."

Priya nodded, her gaze distant. "It's strange, isn't it? To finally feel free."

Anand reached over and placed a hand on hers. "We've earned this, Ma. And we're not going back."

She smiled, her grip tightening around his. "No, we're not

know.

A Future Full of Light

Months turned into years, and the Patel family continued to rebuild. Priya's food stall grew in popularity, earning her a steady income and a loyal customer base. Meera's art was displayed in her school's annual showcase, her confidence shining as brightly as her colors.

Anand's writing gained more recognition, culminating in the publication of his first poetry collection, *Shards of Strength*. At the book's launch event, Priya and Meera sat proudly in the front row, their faces beaming as Anand read aloud from his work.

"Through darkness, we found the light.
Through brokenness, we found our strength.
We are not what happened to us.
We are what we choose to become."

As the audience erupted into applause, Anand felt a quiet sense of peace. Their journey had been painful, but it had brought them here—to a place where hope was no longer a distant dream but a reality they could hold in their hands.

Together, the Patel family faced the future, their scars a testament to their resilience, their hearts full of possibility.

A Future Full of Light

The small balcony of their apartment had become the family's sanctuary. Every evening, after dinner, Priya, Anand, and Meera would sit together, watching the city's lights flicker like stars in the distance. It was a simple ritual, but for the Patel family, it symbolized peace—a rare commodity during the years they had spent walking on eggshells around Rajesh.

One evening, as they sat together, Meera leaned over the railing, her small sketchbook balanced on her knees. "Do you think we'll ever live in a house with a garden?" she asked, her voice soft but hopeful.

Priya exchanged a glance with Anand, a small smile tugging at her lips. "If we work hard, Meera, anything is possible," she said.

The idea of a future unshackled by fear or financial strain felt new, even fragile. But they were beginning to believe in it. Priya's food stall was doing well, and Anand's writing had brought him recognition in the local community. Each step forward felt like a victory.

Anand had been invited to speak at another community event, this time hosted by a nonprofit organization that supported families affected by domestic violence. Standing at the podium, he felt the weight of his journey as he addressed the audience.

"My family and I lived in darkness for years," he began, his voice steady but filled with emotion. "My father's addiction didn't just take his health—it took our peace, our happiness, and for a long time, our hope. But we found strength in each other. We decided that our lives didn't have to be defined by the pain he caused us."

The applause that followed was thunderous, but what stayed with Anand were the faces in the audience—people who had lived through similar struggles, their eyes brimming with understanding and silent gratitude.

Back at home, Priya greeted him with a warm hug. "You're making a difference, Anand," she said. "Your words are helping people."

For the first time, Anand felt a sense of pride not just in himself but in what his family had accomplished together. They were no longer victims—they were survivors, forging a brighter future.